The Giggle Club is a collection of picture books made to put a giggle into early reading. There are funny stories about a contrary mouse, a dancing fox, a turtle with a trumpet, a pig with a ball, a hungry monster, a laughing lobster, an elephant who sneezes away the jungle and lots more! Each of these characters is a member of **The Giggle Club**, but anyone can join: just pick up a **Giggle Club** book, read it and get giggling!

Turn to the checklist on the inside back cover and tick off the Giggle Club books you have read.

First published 1998 by Walker Books Ltd
87 Vauxhall Walk, London SE11 5HJ

2 4 6 8 10 9 7 5 3

This book has been set in Monotype Columbus.

Printed in Hong Kong

British Library Cataloguing in Publication Data
A catalogue record for this book is available
from the British Library.

ISBN 0-7445-5479-9

Birthday Happy, Contrary Mary

Anita Jeram

WALKER BOOKS
AND SUBSIDIARIES
LONDON • BOSTON • SYDNEY

Today was
Contrary Mary's
birthday.
"Happy Birthday!"
said her mum and dad.
"Happy everyday," said
Contrary Mary.
She loved the presents
her mum and dad
gave her.

"Much you very thank!"
she said.

Mary tried out her new stilts – upside down. Then she piled her new farm animals into her new spotty cap and said, "This box makes a good hat."

After lunch Mary
helped her mum
make things for
her birthday tea.
She made inside-out Swiss
cheese sandwiches
and iced all the
little fairy cakes
upside down.

Then she went
upstairs to put
on her party
clothes.

"Come in," Mary's dad said to her friends when they arrived for the party. "We're playing hide-and-seek."

It wasn't hard to find Mary. They played hide-and-seek again and again and Mary was always the one found first.

When they played
musical bumps
and everyone
was dancing to
the music, Contrary Mary
sat on the floor.

Mary's mum brought out her birthday cake.

"*Happy birthday to you!*" everyone sang.

But Contrary Mary did not look happy, not one bit.

Then Contrary Mary's
dad had an idea.

He sang:

"You to birthday, happy
You to birthday, happy
Mary Contrary, birthday happy
You to birthday, happy!"

Contrary Mary laughed
and blew out her candles
and everyone shouted,

"Birthday Happy,
Contrary Mary!"

Giggle Club Jokes! No.16
How do you tell which end of a worm is which?
Tickle its middle and see which end smiles!